EEDOO

EEDOO

BOOK I OF THE EEDOO TRILOGY
SHAROO AWAKENS

W.W. ROWE

Benjamin Slatoff-Burke, Illustrator

LARSON PUBLICATIONS
BURDETT, NEW YORK

ISBN-10: 1-936012-83-9
ISBN-13: 978-1-936012-84-8
eBook: 978-1-936012-85-5
Library of Congress Control Number: 2018947510

Publisher's Cataloging-In-Publication Data
(Prepared by The Donohue Group, Inc.)

Names: Rowe, William Woodin.
Title: Eedoo : Sharoo awakens / W.W. Rowe.
Description: Burdett, New York : Larson Publications, [2018] | Series: Eedoo trilogy ; book 1 | Interest age level: 008-012. | Summary: "Sharoo Awakens begins Rowe's Eedoo trilogy on a Nineday morning under the sapphire-blue sky of a small exotic planet in a parallel universe. Citizens of Broan pray to the One Behind Everything, wear heavy shoes to stay grounded in the low-gravity atmosphere, and honor the Law of Boomerang in how they live. Sharoo, the heroine of this trilogy, is now eleven. Eedoo is a timeless inner presence she trusts completely. It guides her through everything-from stressful situations in school, to the powerful witch Zaura, to service of Broan's king and queen, and to combat with the fierce giant Mygor-champion of the cruel, merciless Glyzeans who want to enslave Broan."-- Provided by publisher.
Identifiers: ISBN 9781936012848 | ISBN 1936012839 | ISBN 9781936012855 (ebook)
Subjects: LCSH: Imaginary places--Juvenile fiction. | Girls--Juvenile fiction. | CYAC: Imaginary places--Fiction. | Girls--Fiction. | GSAFD: Fantasy fiction.
Classification: LCC PZ7.R7953 Ee 2018 | DDC [Fic]--dc23

Published by Larson Publications
4936 NYS Route 414
Burdett, New York 14818 USA

https://larsonpublications.com
28 27 26 25 24 23 22 21 20 19 18
10 9 8 7 6 5 4 3 2 1

DEDICATION

This strange story is dedicated to Paul Brunton, my wife Eleanor, and our granddaughter Katherine.

The tale takes place on Plash, a small, exotic planet in a parallel universe. Any resemblance to other parallel universes is purely coincidental.

As you will see, Plash is a scary and dangerous place. But it boasts some unexpected pleasures, from launching-swings and laffodils to awesome weather and the fantastic Foon. Best of all, wouldn't you like to have a magical Eedoo of your own? Well, someday you may discover that you actually do have something quite similar.

Many thanks to Eleanor and Sylvia Somerville for their numerous helpful suggestions. And thanks to Sophie Miretsky for Bart Filo's best joke.

Thanks also to Christi and Jeff Cox for their essential help.

And I am grateful to Paul Cash for his invaluable insights, wordings, and wisdom.

ONE

It's Nineday morning in Broan, on the planet Plash. The sky is a clear, sapphire blue. Scruffbirds squawk behind purple bushes. Their red eyes sparkle like marbles. They have just laid large white eggs.

Sharoo wakes up, stretches like a leopard, and yawns. She's eleven years old, a skinny girl with big brown eyes and silky yellow hair, long on the sides, with bangs. She's in sixth grade at the Simon Says School.

Sharoo springs from her bed, floats to the floor. Plash is a small planet, so gravity is very weak. The people usually wear heavy shoes.

Sharoo shuffles smoothly to the water room. She quickly completes her water rituals. The girl's face is now pinkish and fresh.

Back in her sleep room, she does a short meditation,

praying to the O.B.E. In Broan, that stands for the One Behind Everything.

She feels relaxed and energized now. "Morning, Eedoo," she whispers into the air above her head.

No answer.

Sharoo puts on her black school uniform. It's missing a silver button. She frowns, shrugs. The gap is down low, so probably no one will notice. She laces up her heavy black shoes.

The girl tilts back her head, listens in her mind. "Thanks, Eedoo," she whispers.

Sharoo shuffles over to the cook room. Morn-meal is already on the table. Jumbled scruffbird eggs, mango juice, hunks of sourbread toast.

"Morning, Roo!" her mama says. "There's banana jam for the toast today. How's Eedoo?"

"Eedoo says there will be a surprise today, from the sky."

"Oh. Well, you'd better take a brella to school."

"She's too old for that imaginary friend, Ida." Sharoo's burly papa stands in the doorway. "High time she grew up."

"Lots of kids have Floaters, Wyfur."

Sharoo's papa snorts. "Not when they're eleven years old! Eedoo is a babyish fantasy."

Sharoo glares. "Eedoo is *real*, daddy."

"Yeah, right. Complete with phony predictions." He playfully swats the air above his daughter's head. "Shoo, Eedoo! Scat!"

Sharoo's eyes narrow. Her mouth firmly sets.

"Don't tease the child, Wyfur. Sometimes Eedoo's predictions are right."

"They're *always* right," Sharoo declares. She gives her papa a cold stare. "Eedoo didn't like that swat, so you'd better watch out. I can't stop my Floater from getting revenge."

Her father gives a rough belly laugh. "Oh, I'm scared to death." He digs into a large bowl of jumbled eggs.

When Sharoo leaves the room, her mother leans across the table. "What on Plash were you thinking? I wish you wouldn't be so hard on Roo. She really believes in Eedoo."

"Humph."

"She does, Wy. Sometimes I can almost feel the Floater's presence myself."

"Humph. Soon you'll be talking to Eedoo, too. Why don't you take the girl to Mrs. Zaura?"

"Maybe I will, Wy. Maybe I will. After all, Roo was born on the day of the Silver Dragon." (In Broan, there are a hundred different signs under whose "influence" a child can be born.)

TWO

Sharoo takes the shortcut through the forest. She carries her notebook, two textbooks, and a folded-up brella.

It's peaceful beneath the tall, purple trees. Orange jailbirds doze on leafy branches. Flutterbys flit festively above honeysuckle blossoms. Little green snapdragons sleep on their stems. The silence is broken only by humming birds and humbugs. They seem to hum in harmony.

"I suppose you meant rain," the girl says, tilting her head back. "But a surprise can mean lots of things."

Eedoo says nothing. Her Floater likes to be mysterious.

"Please," she pleads. "If it's from the sky, it might be . . . an enormous bird. Or a meteor! Or even an alien spaceship. Can you at least give me a hint?"

No reply. Sometimes Eedoo is stubborn.

Sharoo reaches the school grounds. She glances at the two rows of launching-swings, the teeter-totter, the scramble bars. Also at the red metal swing-ring hanging by a rope from a shade tree.

"I didn't do all my homework," she tells the air above her head. "So please pay attention in class."

Eedoo knows all the answers, but sometimes doesn't concentrate.

Sharoo approaches the crowd of kids streaming toward the red brick building. In their black uniforms, they resemble a flock of kid-size crows. Above the double door, a sign says SIMON SAYS SCHOOL in big black letters.

On one side, Clyde Dorz is talking with Mort Leekis. Clyde is frail but handsome, and Sharoo has a crush on him. He has curly black hair and delicate, emerald-green eyes.

She quickly asks Eedoo if Clyde likes her too, but the Floater doesn't answer.

Clyde was born on the day of the Crystal Deer.

"Hi, Roo!" It's her best friend, Milli Potch. Milli reminds Sharoo of a little bird. She has dark hair and tiny dark eyes that don't miss much. "What's new with Eedoo?" Milli was born on the day of the Copper Cat.

Sharoo leans close, whispers. "Eedoo says there will be a surprise today. From the sky!" She brandishes her brella. "But that's all my Floater will say."

The time gong sounds.

The black-uniformed kids jostle and squeeze their way into the school. Sharoo and Milli are swept along by the tide. Sharp elbows fly, and even a fist or two.

Mr. Sade sits behind his desk, silver spectacles

flashing light. Like his students, he wears a black uniform with silver buttons. Mr. Sade's spectacles are square. His head is square. Even his jaw is square. He might seem ruggedly handsome, except for his resemblance to a Spooks' Eve skull-mask.

Mr. Sade used to be a nerve doctor, but some of his patients said he seemed to enjoy their discomfort, and possibly even inflicted unnecessary pain.

"Good day, children of Broan! You must settle down quickly now. We have much work to do." There is a rumor that Mr. Sade was born on the day of the Iron Bat.

Like the other sixth-graders, Sharoo plops down behind her desk. From the corner of her eye, she watches Clyde Dorz. He's so cute, so cool! She tries to tune in to him. Is he aware that she's secretly looking at him? Could he be thinking about her thinking about him? Maybe—

"Sharoo Loo!" Mr. Sade suddenly looms above her. "Why did you bring a brella to school? Maybe you were expecting rain from a clear blue sky?"

All around her, the kids carefully laugh. You'd better laugh at Mr. Sade's jokes, but you'd better not laugh too much! He loves to find fault.

Mr. Sade has a little black box in his desk called a Zapper. It has a red cord that ends in a spread of two bare wires. To punish you, Mr. Sade applies the wires to your hand. The box has a dial to adjust the force of the zap. There's a rumor that he once gave a boy terrible spasms. He couldn't stop shaking for a whole hour! The victim's name was Wadsworth Winkle.

Sharoo doesn't know what to say. "You, uh, never know how the weather might change," she says miserably. "And my Floater said—"

"Idiot! Floaters are a childish fantasy! And the sky is totally blue! Please to stand!"

The room falls deathly silent. Mr. Sade is particularly dangerous when he uses a "to" verb.

Sharoo stands up. The brella clatters to the floor.

The other kids laugh louder this time.

"Silence! That is just what she wants. To make a spectacle!"

His own spectacles gleam. "I know you, Sharoo Loo. You have the innocence of a devious imp!"

He looks her up and down. "What is this? Missing a button on your uniform!" He points at the gap with a trembling finger. "Unforgivable negligence. Please to follow me!"

Mr. Sade strides to his desk, slides open the top drawer, pulls out his little black box. Turning the dial, he smiles grimly.

Sharoo follows him up onto the platform beside the desk. Punishments take place in full view of the other kids, "to instruct their eyes."

"Please to place your left hand, palm up, on my desk beside the Zapper."

Sharoo has to obey. Nothing can save her now!

To the kids, the results of zapping are unpredictable. It depends on what part of which hand the bare wires touch, and how the dial is set. A headache, a pain in your foot . . .

Sharoo looks into Mr. Sade's eyes. He is actually enjoying this! For a moment, his grinning face looks distorted, as in a scarehouse mirror. She blinks her eyes, slowly obeys.

The two wires painfully zap. The girl's free hand flies to her right knee.

Clyde stares in horror. He wishes for some way to inflict a terrible revenge on Mr. Sade.

Sharoo grits her teeth. Her hand feels bad, and her knee is killing her! But she won't give Mr. Sade the satisfaction of seeing her cry. He says tears are for "sniveling weaklings."

"There! Next time you will be zapped on both hands simultaneously, to cause instructive spasms. So. You are warned."

The other kids gasp, thinking of Waddy Winkle.

"Return to your desk!"

It's painful to walk, but Sharoo knows better than to complain. As Mr. Sade says, long-lasting pain is part of the punishment.

Sharoo sits like a statue. "Pay attention, Eedoo," she whispers. "If he calls on me," I'll need your help."

The morning grinds on, and she doesn't get called on. Sharoo is grateful for that. Then the gong rings. It's time for recess.

THREE

Outside the school, the vault of the sky is clear blue, except for a few dolphin-shaped clouds, swooping playfully in the distance.

On Plash, dolphin clouds present a tantalizing mystery. They seem to be alive. Are they ghosts? Alien observers in disguise? Sleek, carefree, almost friendly, they seem to appear and disappear like other clouds.

On the playground, the older kids line up behind the launching-swings. The first ones take off their heavy black shoes and stand on the wooden seats. Soon they are swishing back and forth, higher and higher. Then they jump. Their black-uniformed bodies sail up high in the air, float slowly down. The kids do this over and over, shrieking with pleasure.

Sharoo and bird-like Milli stand to one side. Sharoo tightly grips her brella. Eedoo tells her to be ready now. She quickly opens it.

Clyde is talking to Bart Filo, a chubby boy with a face like a boiled potato. He was born on the day of the Ruby Fox.

"Mr. Sade has a shocking thing in his drawers," says Bart. Clyde thinks for a moment, then laughs nervously.

All of a sudden, a lumpy black cloud hovers above the playground! The kids freeze, strangely hushed. The quiet seems uncanny, almost otherworldly. The black cloud is backlit by eerie light. Wind swirls. Sheets of rain sway like glossy ghosts. They stream slowly down upon the kids.

A flashing lightbolt rips the dark sky. Almost immediately, a thunderboom crashes.

Everyone is drenched except for Sharoo and Milli.

The rain abruptly changes to hail. The hailstones are crystal-clear and shaped like diamonds! They shower down slowly onto the soaked, bewildered kids.

Then the cloud floats away. The sun comes triumphantly out. The little diamond hailstones gleam. The kids scoop them up, shouting with glee. Each clear stone contains a tiny bright, dancing rainbow.

Clyde Dorz is watching Sharoo. He likes her, but he's shy. He shuffles over. "Your Floater was right, Sharoo," he says. "What's its name?"

"Eedoo." Sharoo gives him her best smile, flutters her eyes.

"I wish they were real diamonds," says Sindee Plee, as they slowly melt in her hand.

The gong sounds again.

Back in the classroom, Bart Filo raises his hand. There's a faint smirk on his boiled-potato face.

Mr. Sade looks out over his silver spectacles. "Yes, Bart?"

"My pencil is broken. I tried to write, but it's pointless."

Some of the kids carefully laugh. Will Mr. Sade think that was funny?

Unsmiling, Mr. Sade raises his voice. "Go sharpen it, lunkbrain!"

Bart nods, goes to the sharpener mounted on the wall.

Clyde Dorz raises his hand, cautiously waves it.

"Yes, Clyde?"

"Did you see the rain, Mr. Sade? And the diamond hail? Sharoo's Floater—"

"Silence! That is nonsense. Floaters don't exist. And you are wasting time. We must follow the lesson plan. It calls for geopolitics now. Since you are so anxious to speak, Clyde, what is the capital of Broan?"

Clyde squirms in his seat. He's an intelligent, sensitive boy. He felt Sharoo's punishment as if it were his own knee, and now he's too scared to think. His lower lip quivers. "It's . . . It's . . ."

"The capital of Broan, boy! The capital of our great country!"

Clyde closes his eyes, shudders. "Broan City?"

Mr. Sade looks disappointed. "Correct. But what was it called five centuries ago?"

"F-f-five?"

19

"Yes. Five hundred years ago. What was it called?"

"I . . . don't think we ever learned that."

Mr. Sade smiles a crafty smile. "The same thing, you idiot! Broan City. And what are the names of our royal family?"

That was a mean trick. This is an easy question, but Clyde's brain is now frozen. He's paralyzed with fright. He squeezes his temples with both hands, tries not to scream. "I c-can't r-remember right now."

"Hopeless fool! King Kilgore and Queen Reeya!" Mr. Sade pulls open his desk drawer. "You must be punished!"

Clyde moans, shaking his head. "No," he says in a low voice. "It's not fair!"

Sharoo gapes. She can still feel the Zapper's painful burning in her knee. She can see the anger rising in Mr. Sade's face.

"Don't you sass me, Clyde Dorz! I'll show you what's fair! Please to come here."

Clyde shudders. He marches to the platform like a soldier toy with a key in his back.

"Please to place both your hands, palms up, beside the Zapper. You must have some instructive spasms."

Everyone gasps. The room goes horribly silent. They can hear Clyde's nervous, raspy breathing.

"Do it now! Turn sideways, so the class can see your face. For instruction purposes."

Clyde obeys. His hands lie helplessly on their backs, the fingers slightly trembling.

Mr. Sade, grinning grimly, holds a wire in each hand.

Sharoo feels like she's being punished all over again. Clyde is so frail!

Mr. Sade applies both wires.

The boy's handsome face distorts with pain. As the spasms grow stronger, he lets out a horrible scream.

Clyde's body shivers and shakes for a good ten minutes.

FOUR

Today's mid-meal in the Simon Says cafeteria is especially gloomy and subdued. Clyde's and Sharoo's punishments hang over the kids like terrible black clouds.

Sharoo's knee still aches. She wishes she could eat with Clyde, but each student has a tiny individual table. At least his spasms have stopped.

"NO TALKING. EAT QUIETLY," says a faded sign on the wall. Someone (probably Bart Filo) has added the words "Fart quietly too!"

You must eat everything on your wooden tray. If it isn't empty, you must stay after school to wash windows, mop floors, or work in the well-kept flowerspreads outside.

Today's mid-meal is three things Sharoo hates: cold plumpkin mush, stewed sprouts, and baked scruffbird thighs in a slimy, purple "savory sauce." She almost gags, washing it all down with mango juice.

After mid-meal, the kids crowd around Clyde, even the timid Sparklure twins. He's something of a hero now. He still feels pain, but tries not to show it.

"How bad does it hurt?" asks Mort Leekis.

"I'll live," says Clyde. His jaw trembles. He can barely stand up. "My butt hurts the worst. Like he paddled me, hard."

Sharoo clenches her fists.

"How bad is your knee, Roo?" asks Milli Potch.

"I'll live too," Sharoo replies. She turns to Clyde. "Are you going to tell your parents?" She thinks they both should do the same thing, tell or not tell.

"I *can't* tell," Clyde answers. "If my father finds out how dumb I was, he'll punish me too." He shudders. "What did . . . your Floater Eedoo say, when it warned you about the rain . . . and the diamond hail?"

Sharoo hesitates. Eedoo likes mysterious secrets. But this one has already happened. And anyway, she told Milli. "Eedoo said there would be a surprise, from the sky."

Clyde's eyes widen. He nods solemnly.

She expects the other kids to laugh, but no one does. Instead, they all start whispering. Floaters are sort of like magic, so they're impressed.

"There's another dimension," says Clyde. "One that sorcerers can tune into. Maybe that's where Eedoo comes from."

"The future is already here," says Mort. "I mean, it's somewhere, only we can't see it. Those diamond hailstones were just waiting."

"My daddy said it rained rigglefish just before I was born," Milli declares. "All over the hospital lawn. They were carried by a giant updraft of air."

"I heard about that," says Bart. "Then it rained cats and dogs."

Everyone laughs.

"Then it snowed pegwins," he adds.

"It snowed purple on my fifth birthday," says Milli. "But only at my house. It tasted like grape soda. I caught some in my mouth."

Bart nods. "Most snowmen fall from the sky unassembled."

There are very few laughs, so he tries again. "What's the difference between a snow man and a snow woman?"

Nobody knows.

"Snowballs!" he chortles.

Some of the guys guffaw.

"Oh, gross!" cries Milli.

Bart shrugs. "How about this? What did one snow-man say to the other?" He pauses. "Do you smell carrots?"

Back in the classroom, Clyde and Sharoo sit quietly at their desks. Mr. Sade smiles pointedly at each of them, so the other kids can see.

Then he holds up one finger. "Now it is time for composition. This will be a long one." He grins. "The composition must be at least three thousand words long, so you will have three days to write it. But you must start now . . . so I can check to be certain you are off to a good start."

All the kids groan. Each one tries to think of a topic.

"The topic *for everyone*," Mr. Sade continues, "is *Floaters Are False, Childish, and Stupid.*" He writes it on the blackboard. "Any questions?"

Everyone is looking at Sharoo. Clearly, this is another part of her punishment.

Sharoo herself feels like she's falling through the floor. Or being stabbed in the back with a knife. How can she say anything against Eedoo? She knows her Floater is real. But Mr. Sade is going to check her work! What can she do?

"All right," Mr. Sade says pleasantly. "Begin writing." Sharoo frowns. She sits with her sore knee, staring at the blank, lined page. Maybe she can fake it. Oh, no! Mr. Sade is already walking up and down the aisles, snooping!

Practice your penmanship, Eedoo says in her head. *I'll handle this.*

"Thank you, Eedoo," she whispers. "But how—"

Just do what I said.

She fills up half her paper with difficult words and fancy capital letters.

Before long, a shadow falls across the page. She can smell Mr. Sade's tobacco-laced breath. She can sense his intense interest, his gleaming eyes above her head. She braces for another scolding . . . and another punishment.

"Hmm," Mr. Sade mutters. "Not bad. Not bad at all. Make sure you continue like this, Sharoo." He walks on to peer over Milli's shoulder.

Sharoo can't believe it. "Eedoo!" she breathes. "What did you do?"

I made him see something else.

"Oh, thank you! What was it?"

Exactly what he wanted. Floaters are a ridiculous myth. A silly superstition. A Floater is like a little cloud of ugly, invisible smoke. It has no powers at all.

No powers at all! That's funny. Sharoo giggles behind her hand. "What else did I say?"

That wise grown-ups are quick to see through the deception. I gave him some examples that almost made me sick. He lapped it up.

Sharoo smiles. "Thank you!" she whispers.

FIVE

After school, Sharoo takes the quickcut home through the forest. She's still limping. Her knee feels like it's on fire.

The jailbirds are awake now. And the humbugs are louder. A couple of little green snapdragons snap as she passes them. But she doesn't even notice. She's deep in thought.

If Eedoo can make Mr. Sade see anything it wants, she doesn't need to worry about her composition. Anyway, that's not due for three days. Who knows what might happen by then?

She remembers the story about the man who was paid a thousand gold crowns to make the King's horse talk within a year. When questioned about it, the man replied: "Who knows what might happen within a year? The King might die. I might die. The horse might even talk!"

Well, she thinks, Mr. Sade might die within three days. But wouldn't it be nice to get some revenge on him? Something to make him look stupid or something to give him pain . . .

Clyde seems to like her. Maybe she can plan something with him. But he's so meek and nice. He might not even want to get revenge. He probably still feels pain from the spasms, though . . .

Sharoo's knee aches and throbs. Walking makes it worse. And she was only zapped on one hand! She keeps on limping.

But suddenly her knee loosens up. And soon it doesn't hurt at all! She cautiously reaches down, smiles, tilts her head. "You cured me," she whispers. "Didn't you?"

Yes.

"Thank you!"

You're welcome, but you shouldn't have dropped the brella.

"I know. I was scared. Hey! Could you cure Clyde too?"

No. I am only for you.

Sharoo thinks for a moment. "Does Clyde have a Floater . . . only for him?"

Every person has a Floater. Very young children believe in us, but then they stop.

A tear bulges in Sharoo's eye. "Clyde's still in pain! I know it. Could you please ask his Floater to cure him?"

Eedoo is silent. Her Floater likes to have its mystery.

She prays to the O.B.E. for Clyde to heal quickly.

"Hi, Mama! I'm back!" Sharoo shuffles in the door, pulls off her heavy black shoes. "Daddy! You're home and . . . What's wrong? What happened?"

Her papa sits in his cushy chair with a white bandage on his head. "A log at the sawmill," he says. "It wasn't secured right. A freak accident. Might have been much worse." He sighs. "The logs were supposed to be tied in place, but a big one suddenly began to roll. I didn't see it."

The girl gives him a big, careful hug. A tear rolls down her cheek. "I'm sorry, Daddy. I couldn't do anything to stop it."

"Of course not, honey. It wasn't your—" He freezes, his mouth open, remembering his playful swat at Eedoo.

Sharoo's mother smiles wryly. "I think maybe you'd better apologize to Eedoo, Wy."

The big man stares up into space. His lips tremble. "Please . . . please tell Eedoo I'm sorry, Roo."

The girl's head is tilted back. She's listening hard. "Eedoo already knows, Daddy. It had to happen, Eedoo says. There are many things my Floater can't change. But I think you're even now."

Then her papa picks her up into a big, grateful hug . . . grateful for her, and grateful to be alive.

SIX

Today is Tenday. No school! (On Plash, a week is ten days long.)

Sharoo wakes up lazily. She frowns, recalling a nightmare. Mr. Sade asked her, "What is the name of Queen Reeya's cat?" And when she didn't know, he grinned and said: "She has no cat. You must be punished!"

And then he was standing over her, adjusting the dial on the black box, but suddenly the Zapper was a sword! Mr. Sade roared and growled like a savage beast. She tried to run, but her legs wouldn't move, and she woke up.

What could it mean? Did Eedoo send it?

"Eedoo," she whispers. Are you there?

No answer. She shuffles to the water room.

Observing her head in the mirror, she wonders why her Floater can't even be seen in the glass. "Where are you, Eedoo?" she whispers.

Still no answer. Is Eedoo not here yet this morning? Or is Eedoo always here? Why doesn't her Floater say something? Why is Eedoo so mysterious?

Back in her sleep room, she does a long meditation. She feels her body warmly melt away. She feels closer to Eedoo now.

All of a sudden, Sharoo sees Mr. Sade's grinning face. Clenching her mind, she viciously erases it.

Sharoo prays to the O.B.E. for her papa to heal quickly. Also for Clyde. Those spasms made him shake like a helpless rag doll! She can still hear his horrible scream.

It suddenly occurs to her that she ought to pray for Mr. Sade. He seems to enjoy being cruel! But he's a person too, isn't he? Maybe he was bullied as a child. He needs to be prayed for. She goes through the motions, but doesn't really feel the prayers in her heart.

All of a sudden, she's aware of Eedoo's presence.

Good morning, Roo. It was good to pray for Mr. Sade, but you should have meant it.

"I know, but I just couldn't. He's so cruel!"

Yes. But he is bringing badness upon himself. Like your father did, only much worse. In accordance with The L.O.B.

"What's that?"

The Law of Boomerang. It's very simple. Sooner or later, you get what you give. Good or bad.

Sharoo grows thoughtful. "Did you make the law?"

Oh, no. The O.B.E. set it up. It's beyond my jurisdiction.

"Jurisdiction?"

The things I can control. You think I take revenge, but

I don't need to. The Law takes effect automatically.

"Eedoo! Did you send me a dream?"

No answer. Eedoo goes quiet at the most frustrating times!

So she won't forget, Sharoo sews a new silver button onto her school uniform.

At morn-meal, her papa seems much better. She is grateful for that.

Her mama sips, plunks down her tea mug. "You and I are making a trip today, Roo. To see Mrs. Zaura. Right after the temple service."

The girl almost drops her glass of mango juice. She has heard rumors about the old woman. Mrs. Zaura gives readings. She practices some kind of magic. But the people who dare to visit her don't always get help. Mrs. Potch is still a cripple. And Mr. Leekis is totally blind now. He—

"Don't worry," Sharoo's mama tells her. "Your papa and I think you need to have a reading. There seem to be strange forces around you. We need to know more about them."

Sharoo sighs. "Maybe you're right, Mama." Her parents don't even know that Eedoo healed her! She glances upwards, listens in her mind. "Eedoo says it's probably a good idea, but many different things might happen."

Sharoo wears her white prayer dress, which is too small for her, over some bluepants. She and her parents arrive at the temple just as first-gong sounds. The ancient structure, made of polished bamboo, is rebuilt every three years. This is paid for entirely by taxes. In Broan, it is considered a great blessing to give money, and the King's tax enforcers are merciless.

Inside the temple, people are already sitting on palm-frond prayer mats. Mother Maura, the High Priestess, stands before the Sacred Shelf. She wears white silk robes, trimmed in ermine. Emeralds and rubies glitter from her sleeves and from the tops of her black slippers. Her hair is pulled up in fancy swirls. She's burning vapor-sticks and chanting softly.

Sharoo likes the atmosphere in the temple. The only illumination comes from a glowing red neon sign above the altar that says O.B.E. She and her parents each take a prayer mat from the stack, bow, and sit.

Two-gong shimmers loudly as Mother Maura skill-fully shakes a wooden frame of tiny bells.

Everyone meditates. Sharoo feels right at home. Eedoo never interrupts her meditation, but she can sense her Floater's presence. Eedoo likes it when she meditates and prays. And she feels especially close to her Floater when she does.

Mother Maura keeps intruding on the meditation with instructions about how to pray. And reminders to put donations in the safely locked collection chests. Her soft, sweet voice keeps breaking the peaceful silence by telling everyone to be quiet and generous.

"The O.B.E. knows everything you do," she mur-murs, "including how much money you donate. No

U.F.O.s, please." In Broan, U.F.O. stands for Unfitting Offering.

After a half hour, the tiny bells tingle again. The worshippers come slowly out of their meditation. Then the third gong sounds. The people stand. They return their prayer mats, donate money in personalized envelopes, and shuffle silently out the temple door.

"I'm glad that's over," Sharoo's father mutters. He always fidgets during the service.

"Now, Wy," Sharoo's mother gently reproaches him. "You know it's important to pray. And you always feel better afterwards." She turns to Sharoo. "Now we must go to see Mrs. Zaura."

SEVEN

It's breezy. High in the sky, two shiny-grey dolphin clouds playfully swoop and cavort.

Sharoo has changed to a pink cotton shirt over her tight bluepants. She and her mama follow the dirt road through fields of wild highgrass. They pass purple bushes with sweet yellow berries called "snoots." Scruffbirds squawk behind everpurple trees. On leafy branches, orange jailbirds twitter and tweet.

Soon they hear faint, silly giggles. They're walking by pink laffodil flowers (so named because of the sound their blossoms make when stirred by the wind). The giggles are amazingly human.

"Sounds like somebody's crazy aunt," Sharoo's mother remarks.

Sharoo smiles. She tilts her head back, listens.

"Eedoo says to walk on the other side of the road."

Her mama raises her eyebrows. "A surprise?"

The girl nods. "A bad one. Soon."

"All right. Let's cross over. The road will still take us there."

A few minutes later, nothing has happened. Sharoo's mother sighs. "Well, maybe this time Eedoo didn't—"

She's interrupted by a grinding, crumbling sound, directly across the road. A sinkhole opens up, right where they would have been walking!

"I take it all back," Sharoo's mother murmurs in awe.

"Eedoo is always right," Sharoo declares. She tilts her head back, whispers "Thank you." Then she walks to the hole and peers over the edge. It's so deep, she can't even see the bottom!

For some reason, the girl thinks of Mr. Sade and shudders. A few weeks ago, he told the class that sinkholes are a particular danger in this part of Broan. He seemed to enjoy the frightened expressions on the kids' faces.

Sharoo tosses a rock into the dark chasm. After what seems like forever, she hears a faint, distant *plunk*.

"Careful, dear. The hole might suddenly get bigger."

The girl is still listening. "Eedoo says it's safe now."

"Oh. Well, you've tested it. Let's keep going."

They take smaller roads, then winding dirt paths. Mrs. Zaura lives far from the beaten track.

Sharoo keeps thinking about the old woman. There is a rumor that she helped Mrs. Pilk, who was afraid to go to sleep. Whenever she closed her eyes, she was attacked by evil spirits. And Mrs. Zaura cured her with some eerie magic. She also cured Mr. Larx, who thought he was a ghost.

Some people who have visited the old woman claim that she's in league with dark forces. There was mean, obnoxious Mr. Scrantz, who went to see her and abruptly disappeared. Rumor has it that she somehow sent him to a P.U. (In Broan, that stands for Parallel Universe.)

There were also two little boys who put on scary tiger costumes. They went to visit Mrs. Zaura on Spooks' Eve. They went to scare her on a double dare. The boys were never seen again, but hunters shot two real tigers in the forest, not far from—

"Roo! Watch out for that boa!"

Sharoo dodges as a green snakelike vine swings close to her. On Plash, stealthy boa vines are a big problem. Half-plant, half-reptile, they tightly bind their prey and gradually *absorb* it. Their rubbery skin is sticky and very strong. Hanging from trees, they move slowly except for sudden lunges. Hunters tell terrible tales about finding skeletons beneath them.

"Thanks, mama," Sharoo tells her. "I was daydreaming."

EIGHT

After a while, Sharoo and her mother come to a clearing in the forest. They see a wooden hut with a slanting thatched roof and two dark, star-shaped windows. They look like eyes, Sharoo thinks, and the door could be a nose.

Above the door, an old wooden plaque says READINGS. There isn't any bell or yank-rope. From somewhere inside come three sharp barks.

"We've been announced," Sharoo's mother declares. "Sounds like a yappy little thing."

Sharoo pictures a shaggy mutt with sharp teeth. "I hope he doesn't bite," she says.

The door creaks open. A shadowy head appears. "Yesss?"

Sharoo stares. The old woman resembles a fairytale witch! She wears black robes with silver stars. Her beady green eyes peer out above a curved, warty nose. Her thin mouth, with only one tooth, seems to be laughing.

Sharoo's mama bows slightly. "We have come for a reading," she says.

Mrs. Zaura keeps on smiling. "And you can pay?" She rubs her bony hands together, as if to warm them.

"Yes."

"Come in, please."

She takes them to a small room.

Sharoo gapes. In the center of a round table, a little fire is burning!

She blinks, then sees that the "flames" are really a chunk of fiery red quarzz. It catches the light in a weird, flowing way.

The witch invites them to sit at the table.

Sharoo looks around anxiously. "Where is your dog?" she asks.

"Right here." Mrs. Zaura places her wrinkled hands beside her mouth. She makes three sharp barks. "Like him? His name is Sniffy. Hee hee." She turns to Sharoo's mother. "Is the reading for you or the child?"

"For my daughter. Her name is Sharoo. She's a Silver Dragon."

Mrs. Zaura's eyes light up. "Really? First one I've heard of since Queen Quist." She leans up close to Sharoo. "My! The girl has remarkable vibrations. And an unusual aura." She leans even closer, squints . . .

Her green eyes open wide. "Yee-ak! What's this I see above her head?"

"That's Eedoo!" Sharoo says excitedly. She can't

believe it. "No one has ever seen my Floater!"

The witch's eyes gleam. "Yes, indeed, hee hee. I don't usually see them, but this one is quite distinct. Do you and Eedoo converse?"

Sharoo gulps. "Sort of. I mean, Eedoo thinks things to me, and I whisper back."

"Of course. Eedoo doesn't have a mouth, hee hee. But Eedoo has much power. You must treat your Floater with respect. Eedoo can see into the future, save you from troubles."

"Eedoo just did!" Sharoo says earnestly. "A sinkhole on the roadside."

Her mother nods. "It might have swallowed us up."

"You are a fortunate girl," the old woman muses. "But with great powers come great dangers." She gazes into the fiery quarzz crystal for a minute or two. "You must be forever vigilant."

Sharoo knows pretty much what that means. She needs to beware of people like Mr. Sade. "I'll try," she says. "But I can't always . . ."

"I know," the old woman agrees. "It's a grown-ups' world, and it's not always fair. But with great hardships come great lessons, sometimes hidden. You should always try to learn from adversity. With Eedoo's help, and your vigilance, you will probably be all right."

"Probably?" says Sharoo.

"Yesss." Her single tooth shines as she grins. "It's really up to you. People waste a lot of energy on woe-is-me-ing. Let me see your hand."

The girl places her hand on the table.

45

"Palm up. That's it." Mrs. Zaura bends down, squinting hard.

"I see three moons, aligning to favor you . . ." She leans even closer, as if preparing to sink her lone tooth into Sharoo's palm. "But I also see a dark planet descending . . ."

Sharoo flinches slightly. She flashes on her nightmare about the sword. "You can see moons and planets in my hand?"

The witch cackles. "The palm-lines suggest planets," she says. "And the finger-lines, moons."

Sharoo stares suspiciously. She glances at her mama, who seems convinced.

Mrs. Zaura thinks for a moment, reaches into her black robes, and brings out a handful of silver waxlights. "I will look by the light of the seven fires." She stands the waxlights in a ring of seven little holes in the tabletop. Then she lights them one by one. They seem to interact with the fiery crystal.

"You must both be very quiet," she cautions. "I need to reach a secret U.R.L."

"What's that?" Sharoo asks.

"Ultra-Rarified Level. No more talking now."

The old woman enters a trance. She sways back and forth, chanting. "Castles with their lofty spires, fairest queens, and handsome sires, all are shown by seven fires."

The seven waxlights flicker. Mrs. Zaura blinks and hums. "I see many roads for you, Sharoo, many forking futures . . . Some lead to wonderful, shiny places. Others, to the edge of dark cliffs . . ."

A shudder seems to run through the old woman's body. She opens her green eyes wide. "Yee-ak!" she exclaims. "I see an enormous pair of sandals. How can that be? Surely, your feet won't grow that big. Maybe it's a giant." She turns to Sharoo's mother. "Three gold crowns, please."

Sharoo's mother looks distressed. "I only have two."

The old woman makes a nasty frown. "I gave the girl a reading. There are other ways, unpleasant ways, to make you pay."

Sharoo's mother puts an arm around her daughter. "We just gave at the temple. Please spare us. My husband works hard. Roo is so young . . ."

Sharoo tries to shrink, to seem as young as possible. Mrs. Zaura seemed nice, but now she looks so mean!

The old woman gazes into her fiery red crystal. Her eyes widen, and she smiles. "Yee-ak! I'll just take one crown. Perhaps the girl will pay me the rest one day."

NINE

It's Oneday morning. The sixth-graders troop into class. Mr. Sade sits behind his desk, silver spectacles gleaming beneath the lights.

"Good day, children of Broan! I trust you are ready to learn." His square face leans ominously forward. "Today we shall begin with math."

Sharoo tilts back her head. "What is it, Eedoo?" she whispers.

There will be a surprise for Mr. Sade.

"What kind of surprise?" she breathes.

Eedoo is silent.

Bart Filo raises his hand.

Mr. Sade scowls impatiently. "Yes, Bart?"

The boy smirks. "King Kilgore made a new law. Everyone has to go naked tomorrow. Some people can't bear it!"

A few kids laugh, very carefully.

Mr. Sade opens his desk drawer. "Fool! You think that is clever. But it's not. I must punish you for wasting our valuable time."

The punishing, of course, will waste even more time, but no one dares to mention *that*.

Bart waves his hand again.

"Yes. What is it now?"

Bart smirks, a little desperately. "General Splott called Private Plootch into his office yesterday. Why was this strange?" He pauses. "Generals generally don't see privates privately."

Everyone laughs, except for Carey Dill and the Sparklure twins.

Mr. Sade laughs in spite of himself. "That is actually quite amusing. I'll let you off this time, young man. But you are on warning." He scans the room. "Our math lesson has been delayed. "Milli Potch! How much is seven times eleven?"

Milli's dark eyes brighten. She smiles sweetly. "Seven times eleven is seventy-seven, sir."

Mr. Sade nods. "Correct." A sly smile stretches his square jaw. "If there were sixty cups on a shelf and three fell off, how many would remain?"

Milli tilts her head like a sparrow. She taps on her fingers, grins. "There would be exactly fifty-seven cups, sir."

"Wrong!" thunders Mr. Sade, going purple in the face. "If there were six *tea* cups and three fell off, three would remain!"

Milli's mouth makes an O of horror. Her eyes

are wide. "I'm sorry, Mr. Sade. I misunderstood the question."

"Misunderstood! Don't you dare! That is a Never-Dare Excuse. Mort Leekis, what are the five N.D.E.'s?"

Mort shrinks down in his seat. "L-Laziness, S-Sickness, Daydreaming, Misunderstood the Question, and The D-Dog Ate My Paper, Mr. Sade."

"Correct." He raises a trembling finger. "Milli, you must be punished. Please to step forward."

The kids watch sympathetically. Particularly Clyde and Sharoo.

What is wrong with Mr. Sade? He seems to be on a zapping spree! Maybe he has troubles at home. His wife is said to be a battle-ax.

Milli shuffles up onto the platform at the front of the classroom.

Mr. Sade reaches into his desk drawer.

"Aargh!" he bellows, yanking out his hand.

Something red and squirmy dangles from his point-finger. A poisonous snork! The glowing red lizard has claw-like pincers.

Mr. Sade bangs it again and again on the edge of his desk. Finally the red creature breaks loose, falls to the floor. He grinds it hard beneath his black heel. It makes a sickening, juicy crunch.

Mr. Sade's lips are quivering. "Who did this?" he demands.

No one answers.

He grimaces. Already the poison is beginning to work. "Arraugh." His mouth clamps together like a vise. "My pain is nothing compared to what the student who did this . . . will feel." He grabs one hand with the other. "Do you think I am stupid? There are only . . . two logical suspects. Sharoo and Clyde, who were both recently punished." He pauses, triumphantly grins.

The kids whisper among themselves. They are wondering too. Clyde was zapped on both hands, but he is mild and gentle. Sharoo is spunky and daring, but she wasn't zapped as much. Which one did it?

TEN

"I will not be fooled!" Mr. Sade cries. He blinks. His bespectacled eyes go blurry with pain. "Clyde was punished with spasms. Therefore, it was Clyde! He put the snork in my drawer. Clyde!" he commands. "Please to step forward!" Scowling, he pulls out the dreaded Zapper.

Clyde hobbles awkwardly up onto the platform. He must still be feeling some pain.

Sharoo is horrified. If Clyde has any more spasms, it will rip him apart! There's a thick choke in her throat. He'll go to the hospital. She fights back tears, looks around wildly. The other kids sit like rows of large, lifeless stones. She raises her hand and waves it.

"Yes, Sharoo. What is it?"

"I . . . I did it, Mr. Sade. I put the snork in your desk. Not Clyde."

"You!" Mr. Sade looks furiously down at her. "Well,

please to come forward then." His voice is soft and menacing. He holds the Zapper in his wounded hand.

"No!" cries Clyde. "She didn't!"

"Silence!" Mr. Sade glares. "You won't save her, young man. That's noble of you, though. Return to your seat. That's right. To come up here, Sharoo!"

Bart Filo waves his hand, but Mr. Sade doesn't notice.

Shuffling slowly towards the platform, Sharoo tilts back her head, whispers. "Eedoo, do something! And if you can't, please heal me fast! Please, Eedoo!"

Tell him "Mrs. Filo in the forest" so no one else can hear. Then smile knowingly.

Sharoo nods, whispers "Thank you!" She reaches the platform, stands bravely before Mr. Sade.

"Mr. Sade!" Bart is waving his entire arm now.

Mr. Sade ignores him. He's focused intensely on Sharoo. He stands beside her, tightly gripping the Zapper. "Please to put *both hands* on my desk, palms up, beside the Zapper."

The kids gasp.

Sharoo stares him in the eye. "Mrs. Filo in the forest," she whispers. Her voice is low but clear. She gives him a sly, knowing smile.

As if bitten by another snork, Mr. Sade recoils in horror. But he quickly recovers, clears his throat. "Er, on second thought, perhaps I was a bit hasty. You have shown remarkable honesty and bravery, Sharoo. I know that you won't, um, brag to anyone about my sparing you. Class, take note of this brave, honest girl. Model

56

yourself accordingly. Sharoo, you may return to your seat."

She manages to do so without fainting.

Bart has finally lowered his arm. "Yes, Bart," says Mr. Sade. What was so important?"

The boy looks confused. "I . . . uh, was going to ask you not to punish Sharoo," he mutters. "But you let her go."

"I did indeed, young man." Mr. Sade smiles acidly. "And I have also decided to forgive Milli's mistake. I happen to know that Milli and Sharoo are good friends." He gives Sharoo a meaningful look.

This veiled hint is by no means lost on Sharoo. Impressed by the power of her reference to Mrs. Filo, she resolves to hold the phrase in readiness—in case another need for it arises.

At recess, Clyde hurries over to Sharoo. "You saved me," he says, smiling shyly. "Thank you, Roo. Thank you!"

Sharoo shivers. She sees in his emerald eyes an ocean of gratitude, and maybe even . . . that he *really* likes her.

"You saved me too," says Milli gratefully.

"I got help from Eedoo," she replies. "I can't tell you what."

Bart Filo approaches them. "I was going to confess," he confides in a low voice.

"So *you* did it!" Clyde's mouth drops open.

"Yeah, says Bart. And I woulda got zapped bad. But you stopped him just in time, Roo. How did you do it?"

"Eedoo," she answers simply.

A few other kids gather. Everyone talks about Mr. Sade, and how strangely flustered he seemed.

"I don't think he gave us any homework," says Bart. "What's the ass for tomorrow?"

All the kids laugh nervously, except for Carey Dill. He's not the swiftest mouse in the house. "Is that a joke?" he asks. "I don't get it."

"You'll get it," Bart tells him. "In the end."

ELEVEN

It's a rainy Twoday morning. Sharoo wakes up early. Her composition! It's due today, isn't it? She hasn't written anything more. What will Mr. Sade do when he finds out? She feels horror prickles.

Eedoo will help her. He has to! Maybe he can make blank pages look like writing. "Eedoo!" she loudly whispers into the air. "Will you help me with my composition? Are you there?"

No answer. What can Eedoo be doing? Do Floaters like rain?

It's coming down harder now, about as fast as it can in Plash's low-gravity atmosphere. The path through the forest will be muddy and slippery. Sharoo frowns. Her heavy shoes will get all gunky, and maybe even stick in the mud . . .

Suddenly Eedoo is there, urging her to clear her mind.

Sharoo sits bolt upright in the bed. "Yes, Eedoo. What is it?"

The school will have a surprise today. A dangerous surprise. You must keep all the people out of the building.

"But what is it? How will they believe me?"

Word has spread fast. Your powers are famous already. And Mrs. Zaura has added to your reputation.

"But what about my composition? Will you help me?"

Silence. That is all the Floater will say.

Sharoo does her water rituals. She quickly pulls on her black uniform. A silver button falls off (the same one she recently sewed on), but she doesn't care. She tries a short meditation and prayer, but can't concentrate.

It's still early, so she shuffles to the cook room and makes herself some strong zingberry tea. She munches on a hunk of sourbread, this time with purpleberry jam. She listens to the rain, landing in swirling sheets on the roof.

A dangerous surprise for the school! Should she wake up her parents? No, her papa will be angry. Better to wait.

When Sharoo's mother enters the cook room, she gapes in amazement. "What are you doing up so early, Roo?"

"Eedoo says the school will have a surprise today. We must keep all the people out of the building."

"What! What kind of surprise?"

"A dangerous one. That's all Eedoo would say."

Her papa comes in, rubbing his eyes. She wastes a few precious minutes persuading him, with a tactful reference to his "freak accident" at the sawmill.

Sharoo and her parents work fast. They take turns calling on the teletalker. A few people argue and grumble, but most of them are soon convinced. Many agree to call others.

Sharoo herself calls Milli and Clyde.

"I think it will be a fire," says Milli. "Why can't they just put it out when it happens?" She thinks for a moment. "Hey! Maybe it's a flood, another surprise from the sky. It's raining really hard now."

"I'll bet it's a crazy man," Clyde declares. "With a long-gun. Or even a bomb. You'd better call the badgemen."

Before long, a large crowd gathers on the playfield outside the school. The rain has stopped. The soggy ground steams in the morning sun.

Five mounted badgemen with rifles idle their horses nearby. The principal, Mr. Furgis, and the teachers argue about how far away is safe. The students crowd excitedly around the building, each one hoping to get the best view.

After a quick conference with Eedoo, Sharoo persuades them to move much further away.

It is past time for the Simon Says School to begin, but the red brick building is totally empty . . . except for Mr. Sade.

He refused to heed the stupid warning. "Poppycrock!" he scoffed. "No make-believe Floater is going to control my life! Any student who is absent will be punished!"

Now he sits at his desk, angrily entering the names of missing students into his attendance book. His square silver spectacles gleam in the light.

Suddenly a strange scraping sound can be heard. Mr. Sade looks up from his writing. The classroom walls are cracking! A slab of plaster falls slowly from the ceiling and lands on his desk.

Mr. Sade jumps into the air, floats down. The walls are crumbling faster now. The floor shakes beneath his feet. His eyes bulge like scruffbird eggs. He opens his mouth to yell, but no sound comes out. He drops his pen beside the attendance book. He starts to run.

Then it happens. The crowd standing outside sees the school tremble, sink . . . and then it is gone!

Teachers and students gasp and shout. They stare at the huge, dark hole that has swallowed the entire building.

No more Simon Says School! Even the launching-swings are gone, the teeter-totter, the scramble bars. Only a lone shade tree remains, its red metal swing-ring hanging like an astonished mouth.

Everyone gasps, teachers and students alike. They cautiously back further away.

"Yow!" cries Mort Leekis. "We could have been swallowed up too!"

"Sharoo was right," says Mr. Furgis, the principal. "Her Floater is an amazing being."

"Yes," says Mrs. Rapps, the school nurse. "We were all lucky to escape."

"Except for Mr. Sade," the principal adds.

Bart Filo shuffles over to the edge, peers into the giant chasm, gulps. "Who knew Mr. Sade was a grade-school dropout?"

Some kids nervously laugh. Even a few teachers awkwardly smile.

"We'll never see Mr. Sade again," says Milli Potch. Her pretty, birdlike face is solemn and relieved. "Or his terrible Zapper."

Behind a small everpurple tree, Sharoo and Clyde sneak a few sweet kisses.

Eedoo watches happily.

TWELVE

It's Threeday, but there's no school today. Literally.

Sharoo sleeps late, luxuriously enjoying a warm, extra snooze.

Now she's dozing, half awake. She remembers the school and Mr. Sade. It was The Law of Boomerang! Sooner or later, you get what you give.

She also remembers kissing with Clyde and tries to hold onto the memory like a warm, pleasant dream. He really likes her! And she's famous! Maybe Clyde will come over to see her today, and—

Wake up, lazylimbs!

The girl groggily yawns. She's fully awake now. "What is it, Eedoo?"

There is a carriage on the way. To take you to King Kilgore's castle.

Sharoo gasps. "Carriage? Castle? Why?"

Eedoo remains mysteriously silent.

The girl leaps out of bed, floats slowly down, tries to walk even before her feet touch the floor. King Kilgore! Sending for her!

She quickly pulls on a white cotton shirt and snug bluepants.

Her morning meditation hopelessly swirls with carriages, castles, and kings.

Sharoo gives up. She shuffles to the warm, fragrant cook room. Her parents are finishing a morn-meal of fried scruffbird eggs and toast.

"Guess what?" she blurts, bursting in. "Eedoo says King Kilgore is sending for me!"

Her parents freeze with confusion. King Kilgore was born on the day of the Marble Lion. He treats well those who obey him, but can be cruel to those who do not.

"Why, that's wonderful, dear . . . I think." Sharoo's mother looks anxious. "But why? Will he let you keep living here at home?"

"Eedoo didn't say."

Her father frowns. "Probably not. Probably wants you all to himself. You and your famous Floater."

"Now, Wy. We don't know that yet. Oh dear, Roo! What will you wear? Not your school uniform, I hope. Wait, have some eggs and toast. But not those rags you have on. Here's some mango juice. This is so exciting! When is he sending for you?"

Sharoo shrugs. "Eedoo didn't say that either."

A loud thumping shakes the front door.

The royal carriage, drawn by four horses, speeds along the highroad. It is gold, with a fancy black "B" on the door. Outside its stained-glass windows, oaks and ever-purple trees glide by. Sharoo wonders what the King will think of this plain, simple schoolgirl.

The coachman's name is Zoop. He's a sleepy-looking man with a curly red beard and big hands. He gave Sharoo ten minutes to get ready, but that wasn't nearly enough. She's wearing a ridiculous pink lace blouse of her mama's and the same old bluepants with a red sash. Plus new sandals. Her silky yellow hair has been brushed almost to death.

The girl leans back against the plush leather seat. "Eedoo!" she whispers. "You're with me, aren't you?"

No answer.

Uh-oh. She'll try again later. She hopes her Floater has nothing against castles and kings.

It's a long ride. Sharoo excitedly pictures the castle, knowing she's probably getting it all wrong.

She tries Eedoo again, but her Floater doesn't reply.

As the carriage rounds a curve, she glimpses something bright and gleaming in the distance. It's the castle!

As they draw closer, she gasps. Multicolored banners fly from the ramparts. The turrets are trimmed in gleaming gold. The grey walls shine, like they're studded with real diamonds!

The horses stop on the circular drive, loudly flubbering their nostrils. Zoop swings open the carriage door. Sharoo springs out, floats to the ground. A diving white dolphin cloud almost grazes the top of her head and soars away. Zoop leads her up wide marble steps to a huge gleaming door.

Inside, a stiff, black-uniformed servant takes her down a brightly lit hallway. The walls are lined with oil paintings of previous kings and queens, framed in gold. Eyes peer out from darkened doorways, staring at the famous young girl.

"King Kilgore awaits you, lass," the servant stuffily declares.

The fancy throne room takes her breath way. The King and Queen sit side by side on brilliant gold thrones. They both wear robes of black velvet, trimmed with golden tassels. On their heads rest ornate gold crowns. In Broan, only the royal family is allowed to wear gold.

Sharoo isn't sure how to curtsy. She's only read about it in books. So she timidly approaches the King and bows. "You . . . sent for me, Your Majesty?"

King Kilgore strokes his brown beard. "Yes, Sharoo Loo. I am Kilgore, King of Broan, and this is Queen Reeya." As almost everyone in Broan knows, the Queen was born on the day of the Diamond Eagle. Such people are usually perceptive and kind.

Sharoo says, "I'm very pleased and honored to . . ." She stops short. Should she have said "honored and pleased"?

"And this," the King continues, "is Slybur, the Royal Sorcerer. He is a master of magic spells and potent incantations."

Sharoo tries not to stare as Slybur steps forward. The wizened old man wears long black robes and a silver turban. He looks like he's wearing a wrinkled mask with a white beard. But his harsh eyes glitter. He smiles a cold smile that makes her shiver.

"What is your sign, young lass?" he asks.

Sharoo speaks in a low voice. "I was born on the day of the Silver Dragon."

"That is quite a claim." Slybur's sharp eyes burn. "But anyone can *say* that."

The King raises his carved ivory scepter. "She was, Slybur. I ascertained it with the Keeper of Records."

The sorcerer tugs on his snowy beard. "Records can be falsified, Sire. I think the young wench is a fraud."

He himself is a dangerous fake.

Sharoo looks up. "You're back," she whispers. "Just in time."

Slybur hisses something into the King's ear.

The King shakes his head. "No, I think the Floater is real." He turns to Sharoo. "I have heard impressive things about you. The reason you are here is because our country faces grave peril. The very future of Broan is at stake!"

THIRTEEN

King Kilgore solemnly explains to Sharoo the dire situation. The army of Glyze, from across the Shipshape Sea, has landed on the northern shore of Broan. Their ships fly deep-red flags with smiling bones. They are camped on the far side of the Great Plain, eagerly ready for battle.

"Their army is twice as large as ours," he tells her. "A thousand strong! In the coming battle, we will almost certainly lose." He shudders. "Even Slybur's powerful spells are unable to prevent it. Commander Grast has given us until tomorrow to surrender."

Sharoo glances upward, but Eedoo is silent. "Excuse me, Your Majesty. But can't our sharpshooters pick them off?"

The King's eyes narrow. "Oho! Good thinking, lass. But they have brought their own sharpshooters too.

Our spies have seen rifles, pistols, even cannons and bombs." He scowls darkly.

Slybur leans close to the King's throne. "We are wasting valuable time with this upstart," he whispers.

The King raises his ivory scepter. "Patience, Slybur. We must explore every possible means of defense."

He turns to face Sharoo. "The Glyzeans are a cruel people," he declares. "They worship Blore, the bellicose god of blood and gore. After the battle, they will enslave all of us. They will torture us for fun and amusement. They will force us to work ourselves to death."

Sharoo gasps. "I would never obey them, Your Majesty."

The King looks down at her. "You might . . . if they threatened to torture your parents. Is your Floater . . . as real as they say?"

Sharoo's head fills with scary images of torture. "Yes, Your Majesty. Eedoo can predict the future. My Floater is never wrong."

"Well? What does your Floater say?"

Sharoo looks pleadingly upwards. "Eedoo!" she whispers. "Are you there?"

Silence.

"I'm afraid my Floater's not available now, Your Majesty."

Slybur icily smiles. "The child is clearly a hoax, Sire. There is ample room for such fame-craving upstarts in the royal dungeon."

King Kilgore raises his ivory scepter. "Not so fast, Slybur. I have heard amazing reports about this girl.

They cannot all be wrong. And it was I who sent for her, after all. She should rest now, and we will converse further at eve-meal."

Slybur's eyes burn through the mask of his face. "As you wish, Sire."

Sharoo feels a wave of relief. She stands on her tiptoes, trying to look as old and wise as possible.

The King summons a black-uniformed servant, who leads her to her room.

Sharoo gasps. The polished mahogany four-poster bed could sleep her entire family! She stretches out on the golden spread and dark-blue pillows, but doesn't rest much. Her head is aswim with images of the Glyzean army . . . and of working herself to death.

She tries Eedoo again, but there is no answer. What can her Floater be doing?

FOURTEEN

The glorious dining hall is ablaze with waxlights. Flames even dance and flicker on the diamond chandelier. Sharoo sits beside the King, opposite Queen Reeya. Slybur and General Splott, the King's Chief Minister of War, sit further away.

The King and Queen wear formal black robes with gold buttons as large as cookies! Queen Reeya sports a gold necklace with rubies and pearls around her throat. Their gold crowns gleam.

Sipping wine and slurping his cream of celery soup, King Kilgore turns to Sharoo and declares: "There seems to be only one hope. It is called The Combat of Champions."

Sharoo looks puzzled. "What is that, Your Majesty?"

The King absentmindedly raises his spoon, as if it is his scepter. "I'm about to tell you. Though the Glyzeans are cruel and merciless, they are a strictly honorable people. That is their sole virtue.

"An ancient law stipulates that two warring sides may each select a Champion. The two Champions fight, instead of the two armies. They wear no armor, but can chose three weapons. No guns, of course." The King finds his scepter, raises it. "The idea is to prevent mass bloodshed. It is far more civilized."

Sharoo nods. "I understand, Your Majesty."

"Perhaps you and your Floater, if it, ahem, deigns to be present, can help us to select Broan's Champion. I plan to challenge the Glyzeans tomorrow. I shall propose a Combat of Champions . . . for the next day."

Sharoo smiles hopefully. "I'm sure Eedoo will be happy to help, Your Majesty." Actually, she isn't sure at all, but what else can she say?

Slybur excuses himself from the table, returns with two golden glass goblets. He hands one to Sharoo, "I propose a toast of alliance between two powerful magicians. Assuming you are not a charlatan, of course."

Sharoo looks up. "Eedoo!" she whispers. "Are you there?"

Yes. Tell Slybur you wish to exchange goblets. Make up an excuse.

Sharoo smiles with relief. She looks confidently at the self-proclaimed sorcerer. "This is a great pleasure. I suggest that we exchange goblets."

"What!" The sorcerer's eyes flash. "Sire! This impudent child is challenging my goodwill. To humor her would only encourage her disrespectful audacity!"

King Kilgore turns to Sharoo. "Why do you wish this, girl?"

Sharoo thinks desperately fast. "It . . . is an old custom of trust in my family, Your Majesty."

Slybur angrily glares. Below his silver turban, a drop of perspiration trickles down. "This is a trick, Sire! A ruse to confuse us!"

King Kilgore eyes him suspiciously. "Exchange goblets, Slybur . . . or you yourself will wither away in my darkest dungeon."

Slybur's expression is now strangely calm. Almost too quickly, he hands his goblet to Sharoo, seizing hers. He gives her a piercing, hateful look. "To our alliance," he declares, draining the wine.

Sharoo also drinks deep. The wine burns her nose and throat like a hundred cough medicines! She splutters, trying not to choke. It's much too strong to be wine.

Slybur strangely smiles.

Oh, no! Was the sorcerer acting? Did he somehow foresee what she would ask? Did he himself start with the poisoned goblet?

No, Eedoo would never be fooled!

As if to confirm her conviction, Slybur's hand quivers. His goblet falls, shatters on the marble floor. "At least, it is quick and painless," he mutters, falling after it.

King Kilgore nods grimly. "I always suspected Slybur was a fraud," he says. "He was jealous of your power, Sharoo. And I was tired of his phony spells and parlor tricks." He raises his voice. "Carry out this turbaned piece of garbage!"

As if by magic, two black-uniformed guards step forward and remove Slybur's lifeless body.

"I now proclaim sorcerers out of fashion," Queen Reeya declares.

The strong wine is already befuzzing Sharoo's head. "Eedoo told me to exchange gooblets, Your Moojesties. She blushes, wide-eyed. I mean, Your Majesties."

The Queen smiles. "That wine was too strong for you, dear. You need more eve-meal and a good rest. I think you'll like the sweet mango frost-cake. It's delicious. But we will spare you the zingberry brandy."

Now the King smiles. "I think we all need a happy distraction." He turns his gold-crowned head. "Bring in the Foon!"

"Yes, Sire!" A snooty-looking servant hastens from the room. Soon he returns, leading a small whiskered creature on a silver chain. It's dressed in blue clothes with red buttons, like a circus clown. The animal has the same snooty expression as the servant.

On Plash, a foon is a cross between a fox and a raccoon. Foons are extremely rare and very intelligent. The King is clearly proud of his foon. He gives a signal, and the servant unfastens the chain.

"Foon!" cries the King. "Will you do a little dance for us?"

"Foon!" cries the foon. "Willoo doo uh littul dance furrus?"

Sharoo's mouth drops open. She giggles.

The foon's whiskery mouth drops open. He giggles.

Sharoo laughs merrily.

The foon laughs merrily.

The strange animal stands on his hind legs and bows. Then he dances in circles, juggling two balls of red cloth in his front paws.

Sharoo can't believe it. The foon is so clever and graceful!

She squeals with delight. Startled, the foon drops a red ball. "Careful, Foon," he mutters. "Careful." Picking up the dropped ball with his mouth, he dances backward, juggling once again.

Finally, he stops and bows.

"Well done, Foon!" the King exclaims. He throws the animal a large piece of roast duck.

"Well dumph, foom!" says the foon, munching contentedly.

Sharoo eats a big helping of mango frost-cake. It is indeed sweet and delicious. She is so happy, she almost forgets about the Glyzean army lurking nearby, and the recent attempt on her life.

FIFTEEN

The night is quiet and cool. Sharoo can't sleep at all. Her bedroom opens onto a little balcony. It has a low wall for privacy. There are two lounge chairs and a potted plant.

The girl sits cross-legged on the floor of the balcony. The black sky glimmers with a pale half-moon and cold, lonely stars. She knows exactly how they feel.

Gazing upwards, she recognizes The Fighting Warrior, The Winged Horse, The Little Dripper . . .

At least, the strong wine has finally worn off.

Slybur, she thinks. The L.O.B. You get what you give. It certainly happened fast this time!

She tries to reach Eedoo, but receives no answer. She meditates and prays to the O.B.E.

All of a sudden, she becomes aware of a stealthy, scraping sound. Maybe it's a mouse or a rat, scrabbling behind the potted plant. No, it's lower, like someone quietly scaling the castle wall beneath her balcony.

Very quietly, get the letter-opener from the desk in your room.

"Eedoo! You're back!" she whispers.

Quiet. When a hand appears on top of the balcony wall, stab it! Hard! Your life is in danger.

Sharoo gulps, springs to her feet. Aided by the light of the moon, she gropes on the desktop, quickly finds the opener. It's metal and sharp, in the shape of a dagger. Sneaking on tiptoe back to the balcony, she looks for the hand, but doesn't see it. Yet. But she hears the same stealthy scraping sound. It's closer now.

The moon paints the top of the wall a pale, ghostly silver. The hand should be easy enough to see. She crouches in the shadows behind the solid wall. It's like she's playing deadly hide-and-seek with someone on the other side! The scraping sounds are eerie, purposeful.

Sharoo is almost afraid to breathe. Whoever is coming will expect her to be asleep in bed. Her heart is thumping like a bongo drum. She pictures the large, hairy hand of a fierce warrior, planning to smother her in bed . . . or worse. She trembles, tightly gripping the metal dagger.

Oh, no! A sneeze is rising up inside her nose. With an almost superhuman effort, she stifles it. The scraping sound is very close now.

When the sneaky hand appears, it is silent and smooth. Sharoo pounces. Her dagger pierces it deeply, just beyond the fingers.

She hears a horrible shriek. Through the dagger,

she feels the hand tighten, like a crab, then release. She hears a long, echoing cry fall away from the balcony. This is followed by a heavy thump on the terrace far below.

Well done. Get some sleep now.

"But . . . who was that?"

You'll find out tomorrow.

"I tried to reach you, Eedoo. What were you doing?"

I was observing the Glyzeans. They are indeed formidable and ferocious.

"Will you help me advise the King tomorrow . . . about what warrior to choose?"

Of course. I'm always with you.

"But you said you were—"

I am outside of space and time. Therefore, I can touch more than one place at the same time. Sometimes you think my mind wanders, but it doesn't. I don't try to be mysterious, either. You think I leave you, but I don't. Still, I can't do everything for you. Many things you must do yourself.

"But why?"

You are responsible for your own path. Get some sleep now.

"I'll try."

Get some sleep! That's easy for Eedoo to say! Sharoo shivers.

"Do you know how hard it will be for me to sleep now?" she asks.

No answer.

The girl decides to sleep with her clothes on. She climbs into bed, half expecting that someone will unlock

85

her door and silently enter the room. She vividly imagines a creepy figure with a long, sharp knife.

But no! Eedoo will protect her, won't he? Of course! Eedoo will keep watch. Floaters probably don't need to sleep. They can be forever vigilant, as Mrs. Zaura recommended. So there is nothing to worry about, right? The third time someone tries to kill her will definitely *not* be the charm.

Sharoo sighs with relief. She gets out of bed and jams the straight-backed desk chair under the doorknob. Then she wipes the letter opener clean and places it carefully beneath her pillow.

With teeth chattering, she slips back into bed.

Sleep still eludes her. So Sharoo resorts to the age-old, tried-and-true method of counting scruffbird eggs, shiny white rows and rows of them . . .

SIXTEEN

Sharoo wakes up early, after troubled dreams. It's Fourday, but she hardly cares about that. She shuffles out onto the balcony, looks down over the wall. There's nothing on the terrace below, not even a red spot. Did she imagine the evil hand?

She decides to meditate and pray. It's shivery in the clear morning air.

Soon she feels better.

But she keeps remembering the scary visitor she had last night.

Good morning.

"Morning, Eedoo," she whispers. "Was the hand . . . real?"

Yes. Take more deep breaths. You're still too nervous.

She does.

Sharoo finds the King and Queen in the sunlit morn-meal room. It's lavish, with a splendid view of the countryside. But the Glyzean army, though not visible, is camped not far away.

The girl sips honey-blossom tea, munching on a powdery sweetcrust.

King Kilgore puts his hand on Sharoo's arm. "I must apologize for what happened last night. Perhaps I should have anticipated it. Word spreads fast around here. But I see that you are more resourceful than you appear."

Queen Reeya nods. "How did you know, brave girl? Did your Floater alert you?"

Sharoo understands that they are talking about her nocturnal visitor. "Yes, Your Majesty. Eedoo told me to use the letter-opener from the desk."

"Oh-ho!" the King's eyes grow large. "I wondered how you did it. Well, don't worry. From now on, there will be guards below your window and outside your bedroom door."

"Thank you, Your Majesty. But . . . who was it?"

"Elzo the Great. A circus acrobat. She is, or rather was, Slybur's niece. She will be buried beside him, in a grave of dishonor."

Sharoo's tea sloshes onto the tablecloth. "It was a woman!"

"Yes." The King scowls. "Assassins can be of either sex. She was seeking to avenge her uncle's death."

Sharoo shudders. "But I didn't kill Slybur."

Queen Reeya smiles. "Of course not, dear. He poisoned himself, rather than rot in the dungeon. But that didn't matter to Elzo."

Sharoo tries to mop up her tea, but it has already spread across the tablecloth. "I'm sorry, Your Majesty."

The Queen scoffs. "Clean linen is the least of our worries, brave girl."

A black-uniformed waiter spreads a fresh white cloth over the wet spot, skillfully rearranging the cups and plates.

Another waiter passes trays of exotic fruits, crisp saltmeat, and slices of hard-boiled egg piled with glistening caviar. Sharoo takes a large mango and another sweetcrust. She politely declines the rest. She has flutterbys in her stomach.

"Pardon, Sire. This just arrived." Bowing at the waist, a tall waiter holds out a little silver tray. On it lies a deep-red parchment with smiling bones across the front.

The King snatches up the parchment, scans it.

"Commander Grast has accepted my challenge for a Combat of Champions. The Glyzeans' Champion will be Mygor. I have heard of this powerful warrior. He is said to uproot small trees for amusement!"

Sharoo covers her mouth with her hand.

"But I have three great warriors, Sharoo. You and Eedoo must inspect them and advise me which one to choose."

"Yes, Your Majesty. May I ask a favor?"

"Of course."

"Could I please call my parents? They will be worried."

"Certainly. There is a teletalker just outside this room. Just don't mention the Glyzeans. I don't want my people to become panicky."

"Yes, Your Majesty."

Sharoo finds the teletalker easily, on a low table. The receiver is silver and gold! She tells the operator her home talker number.

"Hi, Mama. I'm at the castle."

"Roo! How are you, dear? Why didn't you call sooner?"

Sharoo hesitates for an instant. She decides not to mention the two attempts on her life. "I've been pretty busy, Mama. But I'm fine."

"I hope so. What did the King want?"

"Oh, just some advice . . . from Eedoo and me."

"What kind of advice?"

"Um, I can't say. But I'm really fine. I have a nice room, and the food is wonderful. My room has a little balcony."

"That's nice. But be careful you don't fall. Balconies can be dangerous."

"I know, Mama." She shivers. "This one has a wall around it."

"Oh. That's good. When will you be coming home?"

"I don't know yet, Mama. I have to go. Please give my love to Papa."

"I will. Call again soon, dear."

"Yes, Mama. Love you, 'bye."

I'll call soon if I'm not a slave, Sharoo thinks.

SEVENTEEN

Outside the castle, Sharoo and King Kilgore sit on golden chairs. General Splott sits just behind them. Three muscular soldiers stand nearby, gripping blunt wooden swords. In accordance with Combat of Champions rules, they wear only long tunics and sandals.

The King gestures with his ivory scepter. "Klaywon, Dargool, Glang. They will fight each other. But not seriously enough to sustain injuries."

Sharoo stares intently at the three warriors.

Klaywon is the tallest. He has shaggy dark hair, a huge nose, and beady eyes.

Dargool is shorter, with stringy red hair and sly, slanting eyes.

Glang is the shortest, with large muscles, a bristly black beard, and a small, quivering mouth.

The three soldiers fight in pairs, different pairs each time. They slash vigorously at each other. Their wooden swords *clank* and *clunk*.

Sometimes one wins, sometimes another.

High in the sky, two grey dolphin clouds happily swoop, as if oblivious to the terrible danger threatening Broan.

Finally the King raises his scepter. "Enough," he says. "Stop, men!" the General commands. "Thank you." All three stand still, dripping with perspiration.

"Well?" The King turns to Sharoo, regarding her with piercing eyes. "What do you and Eedoo think?"

The girl looks upward, listens. "May I please speak frankly, Your Majesty?"

"Of course." The King looks pointedly at the three warriors. "These men will hold nothing against you. We all desire what is best for Broan."

Sharoo nods, takes a deep breath. "Klaywon," she says, "is strong enough, but not very smart. He could be easily tricked. Dargool is smart, but not strong enough. He could be overpowered. And Glang . . . is both smart and strong, but he has a fatal cowardly streak."

King Kilgore groans. "I fear your Floater is right. What then shall we do? Ask him who should fight the mighty Mygor."

Sharoo briefly consults with Eedoo. Her eyes widen. She trembles and gulps.

"Me, Your Majesty." She can't believe she just said this!

"You!" The King drops his scepter. "Surely you are joking?"

General Splott rushes to pick up the scepter.

"No, Your Majesty. Eedoo says I can manage. But I will need a few things."

"In the name of the O.B.E.," says the King. "What things?"

Sharoo listens again, nods. "The use of a carriage, Your Majesty. And a sack with fifty gold crowns."

The King's eyes squint tightly, as if he has a headache. "It shall be done. But your plan had better succeed."

General Splott raises a plump finger. "This is highly irregular, Sire!"

The King shrugs. "Splott, we have no other choice." He turns to Sharoo. "First, the Royal Tailor will measure you for a tunic and leather belt. The sandals you are wearing will be fine."

The royal tailor, Hoop, is a bald man with black-rimmed glasses and a beak-like nose. To Sharoo, he looks like a hawk-owl. A measuring tape dangles from his mouth like a long, writhing worm.

"Please make the tunic a little loose," she tells him. "I'll need to move easily and fast."

Hoop nods. "Sure you know what you're doing?" he asks, measuring. "I've heard tell the Glyzeans have a mighty champion. He'll cut you into nice thin slices."

Sharoo shivers. She doesn't know what to say.

Tell him not to overcharge the King for this. Like he did for the Queen's last party gown.

She does, giving Hoop a cold, piercing look.

"Woo-wee! Did your famous Floater tell you that, lass? I guess maybe you do know what you're doing."

Hoop's hands tremble slightly as he completes the measurements.

EIGHTEEN

In the same gold carriage as before (drawn by the same four horses), Sharoo gives the coachman directions. He is Zoop, the sleepy-looking man with a curly red beard who brought her to the castle.

"Yee-yap!" he cries, and the carriage rolls away.

Along the highroad, purple trees and bushes flash past the stained-glass windows.

When Zoop objects that the dirt path through the forest has become too narrow, she tells him to stop and wait.

Sharoo follows the winding path on foot. She hears the faint giggles of laffodils. At one point, she dodges a stealthy boa vine, swinging from a tall tree. It had moved silently, trying to catch her by surprise.

Before long, the girl sees a familiar hut with its thatched roof and dark, star-shaped windows. She approaches the door, hesitates. Three sharp barks ring out. She smiles to herself.

Mrs. Zaura opens the door, peers out. "Crazy vibrations!" Her lone tooth glimmers as she grins. "It's the lass with the Floater. Come in, my dear."

Sitting at the round table with the fiery red quarzz crystal, Sharoo explains her predicament.

"Suffering auras!" The old woman peers into the air. "Combat against a formidable giant!"

Sharoo places the sack with fifty gold crowns on the table. "Yes. Eedoo says I'll be all right, if you provide me with a few things."

Mrs. Zaura pulls on the drawstring, spies the gold crowns. Her eyes light up brightly. "Freaky futures!"

Sharoo smiles. "Those are for you and your little dog."

"Hee hee hee! Sniffy will eat like the King himself!" She looks up above Sharoo's head. "What do you require, Eedoo?"

"Unh-uh." Sharoo murmurs negatively. "Eedoo says he's only for me, but I'll tell you exactly what my Floater thinks."

The old woman cackles. "As you wish, brave girl."

Sharoo repeats Eedoo's telepathic communications.

"My, my! Powerful selections!"

Sharoo nods. "Can you provide them?"

"I think so, hee hee." Mrs. Zaura leads her to a small back room.

Sharoo gasps. The shadowy walls are covered with shelves. She sees bottles of all sizes filled with herbs, powders, and potions. There are cages and tanks with exotic insects, hissing snakes, glowing snorks. On a long table, she sees waxlights, beakers, and open leather books with yellowed pages.

"Is this where you do . . . magic?"

Mrs. Zaura nods, grinning. "Yesss." She hops spryly around the room, collecting things.

Soon she hands Sharoo a small glass jar. Also two little leather pouches. "The effects of these two will only last about an hour."

Sharoo looks anxious. "Are you sure they're . . . reliable?"

"Reliable? Oh, yes, my dear. I'd bet my life on them, hee hee. As you will soon be betting yours."

"Thank you."

"You're welcome, little lass. Is that all? For all those crowns, you can have something else."

Sharoo looks up, listens. "No, thank you. Eedoo says you could pray to the O.B.E. for me, though. If you believe in that."

The old woman winks. "Why not?" she says, displaying her lone tooth. "Every little bit helps, hee hee! Give my regards to your mother."

"I will," Sharoo replies. *If I'm still alive*, she thinks.

Sharoo returns to the carriage. The coachman is gone! The four horses paw the ground uneasily.

She hears a muffled, struggling sound. Not far away, Zoop hangs from a tall tree, wrapped in the green coils of a large boa vine! His fly is open. She tries not to look, unsuccessfully. He must have stepped into the forest to pee.

"I'll get help!" Sharoo yells. She leaps onto the front of the carriage, stuffs the jar and pouches into her pockets.

Seizing the reins, she cries "Yee-yap!" Fortunately, the four horses obey and run like crazy. She stands in front of the coachman's seat, yellow hair flying. She feels swirls of flutterbys in her tummy. She hopes some-one can save the coachman in time!

Before long, Sharoo rushes into the throne room. Facing the King and Queen, she talks so fast their heads spin.

King Kilgore tries to calm her. "Don't worry," he says. "I'll send six of my fastest riders to cut Zoop down.

At Queen Reeya's command, a servant brings Sharoo a cup of soothing lemon-weed tea.

When the girl recovers her composure, she shows the King and Queen her little glass jar and the two pouches.

"Are you certain these will work?" the King asks her.

"Eedoo thinks they will," she replies.

"They had better." The King frowns. "While you were gone, two scouts from my army crawled across the Great Plain to spy. They saw Mygor exercising. He threw several large men like sacks of grain! And he sliced through small trees with his broadsword, roaring with laughter."

Sharoo's hand flies to her neck. She makes a weak gasp.

Sharoo has eve-meal with the King and Queen. They are all quiet and solemn. No one mentions, or even thinks about, the Foon.

The girl is hungry but also nervous with anticipation. She manages to eat two helpings of roast pheasant and a few boiled potatoes. The gold fork trembles in her hand, and Queen Reeya notices.

"I proclaim you calm and relaxed, young lady," she says.

"Thank you, Your Majesty," Sharoo replies.

And strangely enough, she does feel a little better. She senses Eedoo hovering above her head.

NINETEEN

Long-legged scatterbirds stand on the balcony outside Sharoo's window. They aren't well-named, for they
always fly in tight formations. In Broan, young children
are told that scatterbirds bring babies.

Sharoo wakes up slowly. It's Fiveday, but the girl has
no idea of that. She feels woozy and groggy. She was
unable to sleep for a long time, and finally fell into a
deep slumber. But it's nice that there is no school. She—

Sharoo is suddenly hit by the realization of her plight.
Leaping out of bed, she floats to the polished bedroom
floor. "Eedoo! Are you there?"

The silence is chilling.

"Eedoo! Come back, please!"

*I was observing those scatterbirds. It's really up to you
now.*

Sharoo tenses all over. "I'm too young for this," she
moans. "Hey! You said you are outside of space and

time. Can you see if I'm going to win the combat?"

No. Time is much trickier than space. The future is unbelievably complicated. It has many possibilities because people can choose what they do. But I can see probabilities, and your chances are good.

"But you helped me before. With the composition for Mr. Sade."

Yes. I can make a few small things happen in order to help you. That is partly because you deserve them, partly because you are in touch with me. And I can give you advice, when you listen. But anything major, on your personal path, you must do yourself.

"But I feel so weak and helpless."

Your mind is seasoned and capable. Use it well, and you will be successful.

"Will . . . Will you be with me at the Combat?"

As I said, I'm always with you. But you yourself must do the fighting. So meditate. Breathe slowly, deeply. Clear your mind. You will need to be sharp and alert.

The girl does as Eedoo suggests, praying to the O.B.E.

She feels better.

Bright sunlight floods the royal morn-meal room. Sharoo shuffles in. She's still a little nervous, so she doesn't take much morn-meal. Only a handful of cashews and three cups of strong zingberry tea.

King Kilgore looks worried. "Is that enough? You need to keep your energy up."

"But I need to keep my food down, Your Majesty."

"We understand, brave girl," Queen Reeya tells her.

The King says something to a servant. He bows, leaves, and returns with the coachman. Zoop looks ashamed, but otherwise well, except for some purple bruises on his hands and above his curly red beard.

"Thank you, Sharoo," he says, bowing deeply. "You saved my life."

"I'm glad you're all right now," she tells him.

"Yes." Zoop shudders. "The boa ate through some of my clothes before they cut me down . . . But it didn't hurt me much, praise the O.B.E."

After morn-meal, Sharoo returns to her room for some deep breathing and a last, hopeful meditation prayer. Then she ventures outside.

The royal carriage, with Zoop standing beside it, is waiting to take her, together with the King and Queen, to the Combat of Champions.

The Great Plain has a flat depression near its center, like a wrestling ring. The ground slopes slightly upward around it, creating a large amphitheater. Commander Grast and his lean warriors stand on one side, their faces pinched with hostility. King Kilgore and his army stand anxiously opposite them.

General Splott enters the ring.

"Hear ye, O Glyzeans and Broanians! In lieu of battle, both sides have agreed to a Combat of Champions.

The combatants have been chosen. Their names are Mygor and Sharoo. These two will fight. They are each allowed three weapons, but no firearms.

"If Mygor wins, we Broanians will surrender. If Sharoo wins, all Glyzeans will depart in their ships for Glyze, never to return. We will provide them with food, water, and excellent rum for the journey. These rules are irrevocable."

The general pauses, importantly puffs out his chest. "Let the Combat begin!"

Both armies lean forward expectantly.

TWENTY

The crowd of rowdy Glyzean soldiers abruptly separates. A hush falls over the entire Glyzean army.

Mygor, wearing the required tunic and sandals, struts boldly into the ring. The Broanians gasp. Mygor is a giant, nearly ten feet tall! His matted hair looks like a huge bird's nest. He grins horribly, lets out a savage roar.

The Glyzean army goes wild. They cheer and yell like crazy. Some make uncouth noises and obscene gestures.

The giant's weapons are a broadsword, gripped in his meaty hand, plus two daggers, dangling from each side of his leather belt.

The huge broadsword gleams in the sun. It is murderously sharp! Some of the Glyzean soldiers make bets about whether the girl's severed head will stay perched on her neck or instantly fall to the ground.

Now Sharoo enters the ring.

The Glyzeans snicker and hiss.

The Broanians gasp.

The puny girl is barely five feet tall! She too wears a plain leather tunic and sandals.

An anxious murmur ripples through the Broanian army. Where are Sharoo's weapons? The young girl is unarmed! It will be a slaughter!

But then they notice something glassy and small, clenched in her right fist, and two small leather pouches, hanging from her belt. Everyone whispers. What can these mysterious things contain?

It is known that the girl visited Mrs. Zaura. Did she obtain some magical means to render Mygor weak and soft as a puppy? Did she learn a secret spell to cloud his mind? Has she mastered an incantation to transform him into a toad? Such things are no doubt impossible, but terrified minds clutch at desperate straws of hope.

The combatants stand face to face, or rather, Sharoo's face to Mygor's waist. They are about twenty feet apart. They might be two clowns in a slapstick circus act, but this is deadly serious.

Mygor roars, swinging his sword. With his free hand, he beats his chest like a gorilla-bear.

Sharoo stares in horror. Is this a person . . . or an enormous, savage beast?

Trust me. Remember what I told you.

She glances upwards. "Thank you, Eedoo!"

Mygor flexes his muscles, stamps his feet, snarls impatiently.

Sharoo rushes right at him!

The giant looks surprised. His foe is begging to be slaughtered! He draws back his broadsword, aims at the little running figure.

At the last second, Sharoo dives for his feet! The wind from the sword scatters her silky yellow hair. The Glyzeans mockingly groan. They know that the next mighty swipe will strike home.

Time eerily seems to slow down. When the whistling broadsword hits empty air instead of the expected target, its momentum carries Mygor's arm too far, twisting his body just a little bit sideways. It takes him a crucial moment to recover.

Sharoo's dive has landed her beside the giant's sandals. She quickly opens her little glass jar . . . and sprinkles its contents on the exposed toes of the giant's front foot.

Mygor lets out a shrill, piercing howl. His toes are covered with tiny white ants called "Firebiters." Their bites instantly cause hot, excruciating pain. The giant drops his sword, bends down to scrape the vicious ants away.

His shaggy head is much lower now. Sharoo pries open one of her leather pouches. She flings a grey powder into Mygor's wild-eyed face.

The giant is blinded! He falls to his knees, howling even louder. He gropes for the daggers at his waist, viciously stabs the air beside him!

The Glyzeans desperately shout.

The Broanians desperately gasp.

Quick as a flickersnake, Sharoo sneaks around behind the kneeling giant. Opening the other pouch, she carefully removes a dark object. It is a large thorn, coated with dark-brown, syrupy goo. She reaches out towards Mygor's lower spine, pressing the thorn through his tunic into his flesh.

Immediately, Mygor is paralyzed. His howling mouth stays frozen open. He looks like a terrible, silent statue.

Sharoo dances wildly around him, her little hands clasped in victory above her head.

The Broanian army cheers.

The Glyzean army groans in disgust.

Smiling impishly, Sharoo reaches up and tweaks the bulbous nose of the kneeling statue.

The Broanians gleefully shout.

The Glyzeans hideously scowl.

Then it hits her.

Sharoo staggers. The world is spinning, whooshing like a top. She reaches out with both arms, groping for support. Finding only empty air, she collapses in a limp bundle on the grass. Everything goes dark.

"Doctor!" cries King Kilgore. "Summon Doctor Pondor at once!

General Splott rushes forward. "Stand back, everyone! Make way for Doctor Pondor!"

Sharoo is floating high above a sunny meadow, beside three frolicking dolphin clouds. It's fun to have no weight at all! She swings back and forth, smiling to herself. The air is fresh and cool.

Well done.

"Eedoo! It worked, didn't it?"

Yes. You're with me now.

Sharoo is still floating. She feels a wonderful warm wave of love.

Now she's lying in the purple grass. Someone is kissing her on the cheek. It's the Foon! His face feels fuzzy. She begins to laugh . . .

Opening her eyes, she sees that the Foon is really the long grey beard of a bald man. He's bending over her, holding her wrist.

"She's coming out of it," he says. "The girl will be fine, Sire."

He carefully helps her to sit up.

The world spins, gradually quiets down.

"Sharoo!" the King's voice exclaims. "Sharoo Loo! You have saved the entire country of Broan! What would you like to receive . . . as a royal reward?"

The young girl rises to her feet, sways. She gapes uncertainly.

"Sharoo! Can you hear me? Are you all right?"

TWENTY-ONE

"Sharoo!" the King repeats. "What will you have as a reward?"

The girl is still in shock. She slaps her face, thinks for a moment. "I'd like to call my parents, Your Majesty. And have my own clothes, please. And a full morn-meal. Maybe some of those egg slices with caviar."

"Of course. Ho ho!" King Kilgore shakes with laughter. "But you must think big, little one! You are a national hero now. You must have a generous royal reward! We'll talk about it over a second morn-meal. And after that, I'll send you home in the royal carriage."

Back at the castle, Sharoo uses the same teletalker as before.

"Hi, Mama. I'm all right."

"Roo! What's been happening, dear? How's life at the castle? I'll bet it's pleasant and luxurious."

"I'm all right, Mama. Whatever you hear, remember I'm all right."

"Fine. But you sound a little strange. What happened, dear?"

"It's a long story. I had to fight somebody, and—"

"Oh, dear! Castle intrigue. Please be careful."

"It wasn't that, Mama. I had to fight a Glyzean warrior."

"Roo! Have you been drinking?"

"Not this morning, Mama. I'll tell you everything when I get home. But don't worry. I'm coming home this afternoon."

"That's wonderful! How?"

"King Kilgore is sending me in the royal carriage."

"I remember. The coachman had a big red beard. He didn't give you enough time to get ready."

"He was just obeying orders, Mama. His name is Zoop. He's really very nice. We're good friends now. He took me to see Mrs. Zaura."

"Really. Why?"

"To get some little things. I'll tell you all about it when I see you. Mrs. Zaura sends her regards."

"Thank you. Does the coachman drive too fast? Is he safe?"

"Yes, he's safe now." Sharoo pictures Zoop dangling frantically from the tree. "I've gotten to know him . . . pretty well."

"You hesitated, Roo. I hope he behaved like a gentleman."

"Of course, Mama." She decides not to mention

118

what happened with the boa vine. Her mother might freak out.

"So you're coming home this afternoon?"

"Yes, Mama. But remember. Whatever you hear, I'm fine."

"You don't sound fine, Roo."

"I really am. But I can't keep the King and Queen waiting. Love to you and Papa. 'Bye."

In her white-marble-walled water room, Sharoo takes a gushy shower. She dries herself in a huge blue fluff-cloth. It's warm from hanging near a heater in the wall. She still can't believe the ordeal is over!

Laid out carefully on her bed, she finds the same clothes she wore when she arrived. They have been washed, dried, and folded.

She gets dressed, starts to leave, hesitates.

"Eedoo! Will you help me choose a reward?"

Yes.

TWENTY-TWO

In the royal morn-meal room, as the King and Queen watch, Sharoo stuffs herself full of egg slices with caviar. Then she gobbles down a gooey cinnamon sweetcrust. Then more egg slices. All washed down with mango juice.

"I wondered where your appetite was hiding," says Queen Reeya.

"Yes," King Kilgore agrees. "It's good to see you eat." He smiles. "Now, what will you have as a royal reward? Think big!"

Sharoo looks up, listens, smiles. "Please, Your Majesty. Maybe a hundred gold crowns for my parents?"

The King grins. "A hundred! They shall have a thousand . . . and more when those are gone! Anything else?

"Well, it would be nice to have a new Simon Says School . . . with kind, understanding teachers. And no Zappers."

"It shall be so! Anything else?"

Sharoo listens carefully. Her eyes grow wide. "This may be hard to understand, Your Majesty. I mean, you are very wise, but . . ."

The King's jaw juts forward. "Tell me."

Sharoo takes a deep breath. "Eedoo says that every person has a Floater. Many young children sense this, but they soon forget . . ."

"So?"

"Well, Floaters can help people a lot. Eedoo says Floaters come from the O.B.E."

"From the O.B.E.! Really?"

"Yes. Eedoo gives me good advice, and makes accurate predictions. Eedoo helped me when Mr. Sade zapped me . . . and almost zapped me even worse." She shudders. "My Floater saved many people when the school fell into a sinkhole. And Eedoo did a lot to save Broan."

The King nods gravely. "And what does your Floater propose?"

Sharoo tilts her head back, listens. "Eedoo says to tell you that each person's Floater is like a guardian angel." She pauses, listens again. "Truly getting in touch with your Floater is the greatest happiness you will ever have."

"The greatest?"

"That's what Eedoo says." Sharoo's eyes brighten. "It begins with meditation, and it leads to a deep, inner peace. I'm only partly in touch, but I have a start." A calm, happy expression lights up her face.

"People should get in touch with their Floaters again, Your Majesty. Eedoo can help me show you how. There could even be a meditation class in the new school."

"Oho! Well, all right. We'll give it a try."

"Thank you, Your Majesty. But it won't be easy. Eedoo says most people have denied their Floaters for so long, they think that Floaters don't exist. Eedoo says your Floater is the best part of you."

"The best?"

"Yes! He says the very best. Your Floater connects you with the O.B.E. It is like a ray of light from the sun."

"Hmm." The King thinks for a few moments. "But by means of meditation, people can find their Floaters again?"

Sharoo looks up, listens carefully. "Yes, but it's more like recognizing your Floater, because it is always with you. It takes hold of you . . . when you are ready. When you are pure enough to merge with it."

The King narrows his eyes. "Pure enough?"

"Yes. Eedoo says you need to purify your heart and calm your mind. I'm working hard on that. Eedoo says you must overcome your ego. And pray."

"So Mother Maura can help too?"

Now Sharoo has a strange expression. "Eedoo says she means well, but like most grown-ups, she has denied her Floater. And she likes money too much, like . . . some other people."

"Oho! Eedoo doesn't spare anyone! Is there anything else you would like to have?"

Sharoo tilts back her head, listens. Then she smiles

and squirms. "One more thing, Your Majesty. Eedoo wants you to throw a celebration party."

"What!"

"Eedoo likes parties. My Floater doesn't usually have much fun."

King Kilgore hesitates. "But . . . your Floater is invisible."

Sharoo nods. "Yes, but Eedoo will be there."

King Kilgore shakes his head in bewilderment. "Whatever you wish, Sharoo. Do you have a guest list in mind . . . for the Royal invitations?"

The girl thinks briefly. "Well, my mama and papa, Your Majesty. And my best friend Milli Potch. Also my new best friend Clyde Dorz. And Bart Filo. He's funny."

"Good!" King Kilgore nods. "We could use some more humor around here. I'll make sure that the Foon learns a new trick too. Maybe he will sing a funny song. But what will your Floater do at the party?"

Sharoo looks up, listens, smiles. "Watch. Eedoo likes to watch people make happy fools of themselves."

The King laughs. "Well, I suppose we sometimes do, don't we?"